MR.
TOPSY-TURVY

by Roger Hargreaves

Grosset & Dunlap

Mr. Topsy-Turvy was a funny sort of a fellow.

Everything about him was either upside-down, or inside out, or back to front—topsy-turvy, in fact.

It was all very extraordinary!

And just look at the way Mr. Topsy-Turvy reads a book.

Not only does he read it upside down, but he starts to read it at the back page!

Now, this story is all about the time Mr. Topsy-Turvy came to the town where you and I live.

Nobody is quite sure how Mr. Topsy-Turvy got there, or where he came from, but he did arrive, because somebody saw him getting off the train.

The trouble was, he did it in a topsy-turvy way, and got out the wrong side and fell onto the tracks.

Which really isn't all that surprising, is it?

Inside it's just the same.

Just look at the clock standing on Mr. Topsy-Turvy's mantelpiece.

Isn't that the topsiest-turviest clock you've ever seen?

To give you some idea of how topsy-turvy
Mr. Topsy-Turvy was, you ought to see his house.

The front door is upside-down to start with.

And the curtains hang upside down at the windows.

And just look at that chimney!

All very extraordinary!

When he'd picked himself up and managed to find his way out of the station, Mr. Topsy-Turvy went to a hotel to find a room to spend the night.

The hotel manager tried not to smile when he saw Mr. Topsy-Turvy walk into his hotel carrying his suitcase upside down and with his topsy-turvy hat on his head.

"Good afternoon, sir," he said. "Can I help you?"

Now, something you didn't know about Mr. Topsy-Turvy is the way he speaks.

You see, he sometimes gets things the wrong way round.

"Afternoon good," said Mr. Topsy-Turvy to the hotel manager. "I'd room a like!"

The manager scratched his head. "You mean you'd like a room?" he asked.

"Please yes," replied Mr. Topsy-Turvy.

Eventually the hotel manager managed to work out what Mr. Topsy-Turvy was talking about, and he was taken up in the elevator to a bedroom.

Then Mr. Topsy-Turvy unpacked his suitcase, put on his pajamas, and went to bed.

He was rather tired after traveling from wherever he'd come from.

The following day, Mr. Topsy-Turvy went round the town.

But what a fuss his going round the town caused.

He took a taxi from the hotel, but so confused the taxi driver trying to tell him where he wanted to go, the poor man drove straight into a traffic light.

"Oh dear," said Mr. Topsy-Turvy. "I am sorry very!"

Then he went into a big department store in the middle of the town.

He walked up to one of the counters.

"I'd like a sock of pairs," he said to the lady behind the counter.

"You mean a pair of socks," she smiled, and showed him a pair of bright red socks.

Mr. Topsy-Turvy put them on his hands!

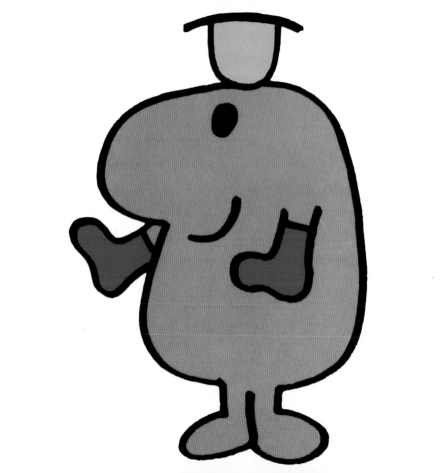

Then he tried to leave, but being Mr. Topsy-Turvy he tried to walk down the up escalator, and all the people who were going up the up escalator all fell over themselves.

It was a terrible topsy-turvy jumble!

He went to a library and put all the books upside down on the shelves, and made everybody extremely angry.

Then he went to an art gallery and insisted on hanging all the pictures upside down so that he could look at them properly.

And then, after Mr. Topsy-Turvy had been in the town for just one day, he disappeared.

Nobody knew how he went, or where he went, but he certainly went because he wasn't there anymore.

The whole town breathed a sigh of relief.

But . . .

What the town discovered, even though
Mr. Topsy-Turvy had left, was that everything
was still topsy-turvy.

"News the is here," shouted the newscasters,
instead of saying, "Here is the news."

"Morning good," people started saying to each
other when they met, and "Do do you how?"
instead of "How do you do?"

Everybody was talking topsy-turvy!

Can you think of something to say that's topsy-turvy?

Go on, try!

GROSSET & DUN
An Imprint of Penguin Random H

Mr. Topsy-Turvy™ and © 1972 THOIP (a SANRIO C
in the United States of America in 2011 as part
by Price Stern Sloan, an imprint of Penguin R
in 2021 by Grosset & Dunlap, an imprint of
GROSSET & DUNLAP is a registered trad
Manufacture

Visit us online at www.p

www.r

The publisher does not have any
responsibility for author or

Box Set ISBN 9780843198355

Can you think of something to say that's topsy-turvy?

Go on, try!

MR. MEN™   LITTLE MISS™

GROSSET & DUNLAP
An Imprint of Penguin Random House LLC, New York

Visit us online at www.penguinrandomhouse.com.

www.mrmen.com

Box Set ISBN 9780843198355   20 19